# Twilight the Unicorn's Sleeptime Quest

JAIME AMOR

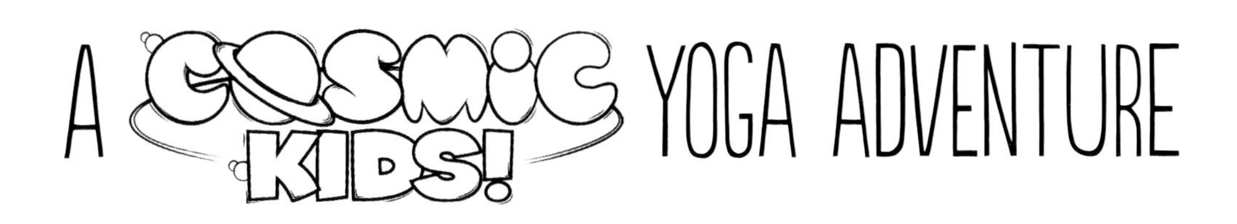

Tonight we are off to visit Twilight the unicorn, who lives in an enchanted forest in the Land of Sleep. Wow!

Just copy the moves in the pictures and enjoy the adventure.

Let's get ready . . .

*Someone's coming on the journey with you! Can you find Betty the bat hiding in every picture?*

*Sit on the floor and cross your legs. Bring your hands together in front of your heart.*

*Now bow forward and say our yoga code word, "Na-ma-stay", which joins us all together.*

# Namaste!

Hello!

We need to get ready for a night-time adventure in the Land of Sleep. So let's try some special night-time **stretches**.

*Stand up and reach to the sky. Wave your hands and say, "Hello, night!"*

Hello, night!

*Lean over to one side and make a half-moon shape.*

Then bend to the other side, feeling a lovely stretch all the way down your body.

Now let's make it a full moon. Step your legs wide, cup your hands around your mouth and blow.

Hello, moon!

Stretch your arms out wide, with your hands up, and bend your knees . . . Make your moon big and round!

*Now stretch your legs and arms to make yourself into a star.*

*Twinkle your fingertips to add a bit of sparkle.*

Oh look, here come some woozy, sleepy **sheep**! They are going to lead us to the Land of Sleep.

*Then lift your knees off the ground and wiggle your bottom from side to side.*

We follow the sheep and, when they reach a fence, they **bounce** over it . . .

*Bounce over the fence like a sheep! Press your feet and hands into the floor and lift your bottom to the sky, going "Baaa".*

*Come down to your knees and bounce up again, and again, and again . . .*

Baa! Baaa! Baaaa!

Wow! The sheep have brought us to the forest where Twilight lives. Look at all the magical trees and strange, sleepy plants.

In front of us is a very **crooked tree**.

*Stand tall, with your feet together. Spread your arms out wide like branches.*

*Bend your knees to make a crooked trunk.*

*Keep your feet where they are and turn your body to the side.*

*Can you be a crooked tree on the other side?*

How will we find Twilight the unicorn?

Let's **climb** up to see if we can spot her.

*Standing tall, reach up the tree with one arm and the opposite leg, then with the other arm and leg . . .*

**Up we go, up we go!**

We get halfway up the tree
but we still can't see Twilight.

So we **climb** a bit higher . . .

When we get close to the top of the tree, we take a look through our night **goggles** to see better.

*Join your thumbs and fingers together and have a look through.*

Suddenly a baby **owl** tumbles off a branch and lands in front of us.

**Too-wit too-woo...**

"Hello!" she says. "My name is Tallulah." She's so sweet! Then she whispers,

*"Twilight is waiting for yooo.*
*She doesn't know what to dooo.*
*She can't get to sleep,*
*She fears dreaming, you see . . .*
*Maybe you can give her a clue?"*

It sounds like Twilight can't find her starshine! Whenever a bad dream comes along, our starshine makes it go away.

Tallulah says, "Don't worry. You can help Twilight look for her starshine!"

*To fly like an owl, start by kneeling with your arms down.*

*Then lift up off your heels, reaching your wings out to the side and up above your head. Too-wit!*

*Swoop your arms down as you lower back down on your heels. Too-woo!*

*Lift and lower a few times as you say, "Too-wit, too-woo!"*

## Too-wit too-woo...

We ask our new friend Tallulah if she will take us to Twilight. We don't want to get lost in this spooky enchanted forest . . .

Tallulah tells us that we can fly just like her in the magical Land of Sleep! She shows us what to do . . .

. . . and off we go, flapping our **wings**.

*Fly like a bird. Fold forward, keeping your back straight and long.*

*Stretch your arms out wide like wings.*

*Gently flap your wings down to the ground and then back up. Pull in your tummy to support your back.*

*Flap your wings 3 times and then soar on the wind . . . Hold your arms out wide for a moment. Then start flapping them again. Repeat 3 times.*

With Tallulah beside us, we fly through the purple, starry sky above the treetops.

Soon we see a lake below us.

Too-wit too-woo...

Our **owl** friend flies down to land and we come down next to her.

*Kneel with your wings down.*

*Lift up off your heels, flapping your wings out to the side and above your head. Lift and lower your arms a few times.*

We thank Tallulah and say, **"Namaste!"**

*Sitting with your legs crossed, bring your hands together in front of your heart. Bend forward and say, "Na-ma-stay".*

Tallulah swoops off silently into the night.

The **lake** sparkles in the moonlight, shimmering and twinkling.

*Put the soles of your feet together to make a wide diamond-shaped lake with your legs.*

The water is as clear as a mirror and we look down to see our reflection.

*Hold your feet and fold your body forward to look into the water.*

Suddenly we hear a sound . . .

Clip clop! Clip clop!

Clip clop! Clip clop!

It's Twilight the **unicorn**!

**Hello, Twilight!**

Twilight says, "I'm so pleased you are here."
But she looks really upset!
"It's terrible!" she wails. "I can't get to sleep.
I'm frightened of having bad dreams."

Poor Twilight! She needs to sleep –
everybody does. That's how we grow,
stay strong and enjoy every day.

*Kneel down and bring one foot forward so your knee is up. Lift your arms above your head like a unicorn's horn.*

*Rock forward, then look up and lift your heart to the sky. Straighten up as you rock back.*

*Keep rocking forward and back, making a clip clop noise.*

Clip clop! Clip clop!

We need to help Twilight find her **starshine** so she can get a good night's sleep and feel safe in her dreams. Luckily we know where ours is . . .

. . . and we become more peaceful as the starshine starts to work.

*To feel your starshine, kneel down and place one hand on your heart and one hand on your tummy.*

The starshine makes us feel sleepy, so we close our eyes and **breathe** slowly.

*As you sit on your heels, count down slowly from 10 to 1.*

*Aaah!*

*At the end, take a big deep breath in and out.*

"See, Twilight?" we say.
"It's important to find our starshine . . .
It keeps us safe in our dreams and helps us sleep all night long."

But poor Twilight just can't find her starshine. She's too upset to stay still and starts clip clopping about again.

"Oh, why can't I find my starshine!" wails our **unicorn** friend.

*Be a unicorn on your other side.*

*Kneel down and bring one foot forward. Lift your arms like a unicorn horn and rock backward and forward.*

Suddenly, we have an idea.

"Twilight, let's ask the other animals in the forest where their starshine lives. Maybe they can help you find yours . . ."

"That's a great idea!" says Twilight. She leads us deep into the forest to a tiny **house**.

*To make a house, jump your feet wide and point your toes forward.*

*Stretch your arms out wide and then lift them above your head. Bring your hands together to make a pointy roof.*

Inside the house is Matilda the **mouse**.

*Kneel down and fold forward with your arms down by your sides. Tuck your head into your knees and squeak like a mouse!*

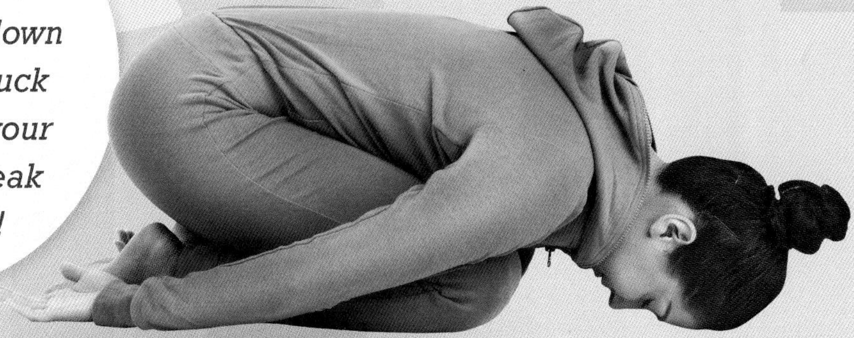

Matilda has lots of little baby mice who never want to go to sleep.

Can you see them bouncing on the **bed**?

*Make a bed. Sit on your bottom and bend your knees, keeping your feet flat on the ground.*

*Place your hands behind you with your fingers pointing toward your bottom.*

*Press into your feet and lift your hips.*

*Bounce with the mice! Jump up and come down to land in a crouch.*

The baby mice are **jumping** and having lots of fun.
We want to join in!

**Boing, boing, boing!**

When we have had enough of jumping, we ask Matilda, "So how do you manage to get your babies to sleep?"

*Bounce a few times!*

Matilda shows us a tiny **jug**.

“I keep my starshine in here. When it’s time for bed, I mix it with some milk or water for my babies. Then I read them a goodnight story and the starshine helps them feel ready for sleep.”

Matilda pours some more starshine out of her jug and all her baby mice fall asleep.

What a good idea! A drink and a book at bedtime will really help us feel sleepy – and the story might even become part of our dreams.

“Thank you, Matilda!” we whisper as we tiptoe away quietly.

*To be a jug, stand up, put your heels together and bend your knees outward.*

*Then put one hand on your hip to make a handle and the other out to the side to make a spout.*

*Can you be a jug on the other side?*

Not far from Matilda's house, there is a large **hole** in the ground.
It must be someone's burrow. We take a peek inside . . .

*Sit with your knees wide and your feet touching to make a diamond shape. Fold forward to look into the burrow.*

All of a sudden Mr Hoppit the hare **hops** out!

*Crouch down and put your hands down flat in front of you.*

*Lift your bottom a little, then hop your feet up.*

*Have fun doing a few hare hops.*

*Kneel and clasp your hands behind your back. Fold forward and lift up your long hare ears.*

Mr Hoppit the hare sits down. He has very long **ears** that twitch as he speaks.

Mr Hoppit also has lots of babies.
The little hares are all running around laughing and playing with their carrots.

It looks like fun and we decide to join in!

*Stand up tall and straight like a carrot.*

*Can you be a happy, smiling carrot?*

*. . . a sad carrot with your shoulders hunched up?*

*. . . a cross carrot?*

*. . . a disco-dancing carrot shaking it all about?*

When we have caught our breath, Mr Hoppit explains, "Us hares get all our starshine from carrots.

"When it's time for bed, I give each of my children a carrot. Then we listen to some lovely songs sung by the night birds."

*To tweet like a bird, come up onto your knees and stretch your arms out wide.*

*Then wrap your arms around your shoulders. Tweet your elbows up and down.*

"Then we all **snuggle** down together."

*Kneel down and stretch your arms out behind you.*

What brilliant ideas from Mr Hoppit the hare!

Twilight can try all these things – a drink or a snack before bed, a story, listening to some relaxing music and then snuggling down.

All these ideas should help Twilight feel nice and sleepy. But will she find her own starshine so she can enjoy sweet dreams?

Just then our friend Tallulah the **owl** swoops down out of the sky. She has come to see how we are getting on with Twilight . . .

Too-wit too-woo...

*Kneel with your wings down by your side.*

*Lift up off your heels, flapping your wings out to the side and above your head.*

*Lift and lower your arms a few times.*

Tallulah comes to **land** on a branch.

*Land like Tallulah. From standing, jump up and come down to land in a crouch.*

All of sudden she notices something . . .

"Look, Twilight – your horn is twinkling in the moonlight!" she says. "Maybe that's where your starshine is."

# TWILIGHT'S SONG Starshine!

In the middle of the night I wake with a fright
And I can't get back to sleep.
Dreams stuck in my head and monsters under the bed
I hide my head beneath the sheets.

Starshine, starshine, sparkle over me!
Keep me safe and sound as I get a good night's sleep.
Starshine, starshine, take me to my dreams,
Show me to the rainbow's end where the river meets the sea.

Let my dreams stay big and my worries stay small
And sleep will take care of the rest.
The happiest nights are when there's no need to fight
And in the morning I will be at my best.

'Cos now I know how to take
the time to sleep so peacefully . . .
I close my eyes, let my worries go
and I slowly, slowly breathe.

Starshine, starshine, sparkle over me!
Keep me safe and sound as I get a good night's sleep.
Starshine, starshine, take me to my dreams,
Show me to the rainbow's end where the river meets the sea.

*Kneel down and bring one foot forward so your knee is up.*

Our beautiful **unicorn** friend stretches, reaching her horn up into the moonlight. Tallulah is right, her horn is twinkling!

*Lift your arms above your head like a unicorn's horn. Rock forward and back, and make a clip clop sound.*

Clip clop!
Clip clop!

Then she bows forward pointing her horn down.

*Keep your arms above your head and bend forward.*

A rainbow of sparkling starshine whooshes from the tip of her magical horn.

That's it! She has found her starshine!

Now Twilight knows where her starshine is, she can use it, along with all those other wonderful bedtime ideas, to enjoy being asleep and have lovely dreams every night.

Twilight is so happy!

She blows us a **kiss**.

Her special starshine **sprinkles** over us.

*Use your fingertips to pitter patter all over your head like raindrops.*

We have helped Twilight find her starshine and it's time to go home. We give her a **cuddle** and say goodbye.

*Come up on your knees and stretch your arms out wide.*

*Then wrap them around your shoulders in a nice, big hug.*

Twilight says, "Thank you for helping me find my starshine. I will never need to worry about bedtime again!"

She's right! All you have to do is close your eyes, relax your mind and let go of your worries. We can't wait to try it tonight . . .

Look, a **magic carpet** has arrived to take us home!

We get on and it lifts off, gently carrying us away.

*Sit up with your legs wide.*

*Reaching to the side, then forward, then to the other side and then backward, swirl from your waist in a circle, first one way a few times . . .*

*. . . then the other way!*

We lie back on the carpet as it soars through the sky. The stars shining in the sky are too bright, so we blow them all out as if they were **candles**.

*Lie flat on your back, arms wide. Lift your legs up to the sky.*

*Your toes wiggle like flickering candle flames. Can you blow them all out?*

Then we lie back quietly.
Our eyes feel heavy and close slowly . . .

As we relax, let's think about
our amazing adventure with Twilight.

*Lie down comfortably on your back, your feet apart and your arms a little away from your sides.*

*Feel your arms and legs become heavy and long. Melt into the ground and close your eyes to enjoy a rest and think about the yoga adventure you have been on.*

Our dreams can take us wherever we want to go, but no matter what happens in a dream, we are always safe.

After a good sleep, we wake up wiser and stronger. So let's use the starshine in our bodies to feel settled and relaxed. Our starshine will help us sleep through the whole night in our own beds, feeling peaceful, happy and safe.

This is an affirmation. Affirmations are good and helpful thoughts that we say out loud.

When we say an affirmation, we make it come alive – like planting a seed and giving it sunshine and water. Then it grows into something big and strong that will help us in our life.

Thoughts can be very powerful things. When we turn them into affirmations they become even stronger.

*As you lie on the floor, put one hand on your chest and one hand on your tummy and try saying the affirmation out loud.*

*Believe the words as you say them and they will grow stronger and stronger, until they are part of who you are.*

*Repeat the words a few times out loud. It doesn't have to be more than a whisper.*

## "I am peaceful and ready to go to sleep."

# "I am safe in my dreams."

*Twilight also likes this affirmation. You can copy her or make up some good ones of your own.*

We rest quietly in this peaceful time.
We have learned so much and
we have made such lovely friends,
especially Twilight the unicorn!

It's time to end our yoga adventure,
so let's sit up like we did at the beginning.

*Did you find Betty the bat
hiding in every picture?*

*Slowly start to wiggle your fingers and toes. Have a little stretch and then roll over to one side. Sit up slowly and cross your legs.*

*Bring your hands to your heart and bow forward, saying our special yoga code word, "Na-ma-stay".*

# **Namaste!** Goodbye!

# Jaime's top tips for using the Cosmic Kids books

Grown-ups, here are a few tips for helping children get the most out of the Cosmic Kids adventure books. It doesn't matter if you don't practise yoga yourself, you can still encourage your children to have a go at the poses – and you might want to have some fun trying them out yourself!

## Read the story, copy the moves and enjoy the adventure

This is an active book that encourages children to act out the story by doing the yoga moves. It's a lot of fun and provides children with a great, balanced yoga routine. They can come back to the book again and again, becoming more skilled and eventually developing their own yoga practice. After going on the yoga adventure a few times, they may even be able to do the whole routine, with all the poses in order, without looking at the book!

## Start by reading the story and looking at the pictures

Being able to visualize the characters and understand what's happening in the story will help children as they try out the yoga moves.

## Use a yoga mat (or a towel)

A yoga mat gives a soft surface to lie on, as well as a defined space to practise in. Plus it makes it feel like "proper" yoga! If you don't have a mat, try using a rug or a big towel.

## Taking part is more important than getting it right

Even though all the yoga poses in the book are adapted from traditional "adult" yoga, the key is to make the experience as fun and playful for children as possible. So rather than stopping them to correct their poses, it's best to let the children interpret what they see and read and have fun making the shapes of the poses. With practice, as they re-read and look at the pictures again, they will become more accurate. The main goal is for them to enjoy the yoga!

## Try to do each pose on both sides

This helps to keep the body in balance.

## Join in to help the kids get the most out of their yoga adventure

- Make the animal noises! Encouraging the children to make fun sounds while they do the moves helps remind them of the poses.
- Get the children to come up with extra ideas for the story – for example, you could ask them where Tallulah lives or what Matilda's babies are called.
- Bring the poses into everyday life. It's always a good time for flying like an owl! Or you might want to clip clop like Twilight, hop like Mr Hoppit or do a crazy carrot dance . . .

## Talk about the story

Each Cosmic Kids adventure offers practical advice for dealing with a particular issue. It's really useful to talk to your children about what they learned from the story so they have some ideas and techniques available when similar situations occur in real life. Ask the children if they can relate to any of the characters in the story and what they would do if something like that happened to them. Twilight discovers that anyone can have problems going to sleep – and also that the answer is inside all of us. If we can find our starshine, we'll have lovely dreams that allow us to sleep peacefully in our own beds all through the night. Twilight also finds other solutions for relaxing at bedtime, such as a good story or a hot drink.

## Practise the affirmations

These short statements are handy tools for daily life, helping to provide instant calm and also to sow the seeds for positive change (see pages 42–3).

## Try out the video

You can watch and practise with me on the Cosmic Kids YouTube channel – access Twilight's adventure and many others via my website: www.cosmickids.com

## Watch out for more Cosmic Kids books . . .

There are lots more yoga adventures to be had. You can dive down to the bottom of the ocean and help Norris the seahorse face up to the bullies. You can travel to Africa and help Lulu the lion cub learn to roar. And Sheriff Updown the rabbit is in a spot of bother with the bandits – can his amazing Zappy Happy save the day?

## About Cosmic Kids

Jaime and Martin Amor are a husband-and-wife team from Henley-on-Thames who run Cosmic Kids with the aim of making yoga and mindfulness fun for kids. It all began in their local village hall in 2012, when they filmed a "yoga adventure" Jaime had been sharing in her yoga classes in nearby schools. This was the first of many videos posted to YouTube and now – many monthly episodes later – millions of kids worldwide have discovered yoga and mindfulness through the free videos. Every Cosmic Kids yoga adventure is written to help kids learn a simple lesson for a happy life, so that they understand themselves and the world around them a little better.

To have more fun with Cosmic Kids, visit **cosmickids.com**!

**Twilight the Unicorn's Sleeptime Quest**
Jaime Amor

First published in the UK and USA in 2017 by
Watkins, an imprint of Watkins Media Limited
19 Cecil Court
London WC2N 4EZ

enquiries@watkinspublishing.com



Publisher: Jo Lal
Development Editor: Fiona Robertson
Editor: Simona Sideri
Head of Design: Georgina Hewitt
Designer and Picture Research: Jade Wheaton
Production: Uzma Taj
Commissioned Illustration: Nick Hilditch
Commissioned Photography: David Lloyd

A CIP record for this book is available from the British Library

ISBN: 978-1-78028-959-5

10 9 8 7 6 5 4 3 2 1

Typeset in Museo Sans Rounded, Rockwell and Caviar Dreams
Colour reproduction by XY Digital, UK
Printed in China

www.watkinspublishing.com